TULSA CITY-COUNTY LIBRARY

W9-BHS-970

JAN - - 2018

Dear Parents:

Congratulations! Your child is taking the first steps on an exciting journey. The destination? Independent reading!

STEP INTO READING® will help your child get there. The program offers five steps to reading success. Each step includes fun stories and colorful art or photographs. In addition to original fiction and books with favorite characters, there are Step into Reading Non-Fiction Readers, Phonics Readers and Boxed Sets, Sticker Readers, and Comic Readers—a complete literacy program with something to interest every child.

Learning to Read, Step by Step!

Ready to Read   Preschool–Kindergarten
• big type and easy words • rhyme and rhythm • picture clues
For children who know the alphabet and are eager to begin reading.

Reading with Help   Preschool–Grade 1
• basic vocabulary • short sentences • simple stories
For children who recognize familiar words and sound out new words with help.

Reading on Your Own   Grades 1–3
• engaging characters • easy-to-follow plots • popular topics
For children who are ready to read on their own.

Reading Paragraphs   Grades 2–3
• challenging vocabulary • short paragraphs • exciting stories
For newly independent readers who read simple sentences with confidence.

Ready for Chapters   Grades 2–4
• chapters • longer paragraphs • full-color art
For children who want to take the plunge into chapter books but still like colorful pictures.

STEP INTO READING® is designed to give every child a successful reading experience. The grade levels are only guides; children will progress through the steps at their own speed, developing confidence in their reading.

Remember, a lifetime love of reading starts with a single step!

For Alex Smith,
who can do anything
—C.C.

Copyright © 2018 DC Comics. DC SUPER HERO GIRLS and all
related characters and elements © & ™ DC Comics and Warner Bros.
Entertainment Inc. WB SHIELD: ™ & © WBEI. (s18)
RHUS39675

All rights reserved. Published in the United States by Random House Children's Books, a division
of Penguin Random House LLC, 1745 Broadway, New York, NY 10019, and in Canada by Penguin
Random House Canada Limited, Toronto.

Step into Reading, Random House, and the Random House colophon are registered trademarks of
Penguin Random House LLC.

Visit us on the Web!
StepIntoReading.com
rhcbooks.com
dcsuperherogirls.com
dckids.com

ISBN 978-1-5247-6917-8 (trade) – ISBN 978-1-5247-6918-5 (lib. bdg.)
ISBN 978-1-5247-6919-2 (ebook)

Printed in the United States of America

10 9 8 7 6 5 4 3 2 1

Butterfly Battle!

by Courtney Carbone

illustrated by Pernille Ørum-Nielsen

Random House 🏠 New York

It was a bright, sunny day
at Super Hero High School.
The young hero Bumblebee
was giving a presentation
in science class
about alien butterflies.

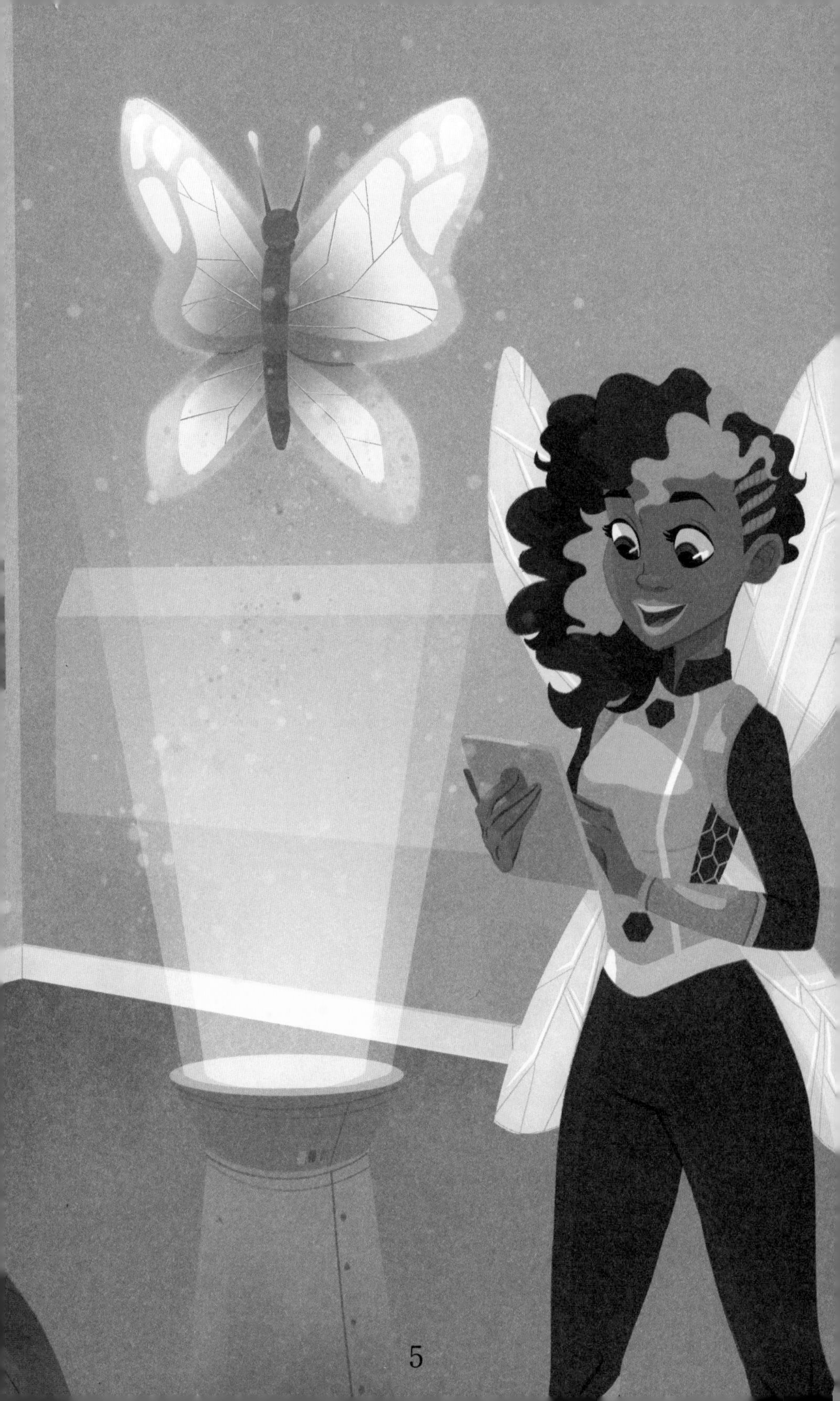

"Space monarchs migrate across our solar system as part of their life cycle," she explained. "They visit Earth once every hundred years.

"My research shows that
they'll be landing in Metropolis
this week!"
Everyone was excited.

Word spread quickly,
and people from all over
came to see the butterflies.

"I think I see one!" Batgirl cried.
But it was just Beast Boy
having a little fun.

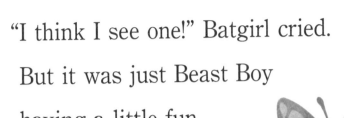

Then, just as predicted,
hundreds of space monarchs
landed near the school!

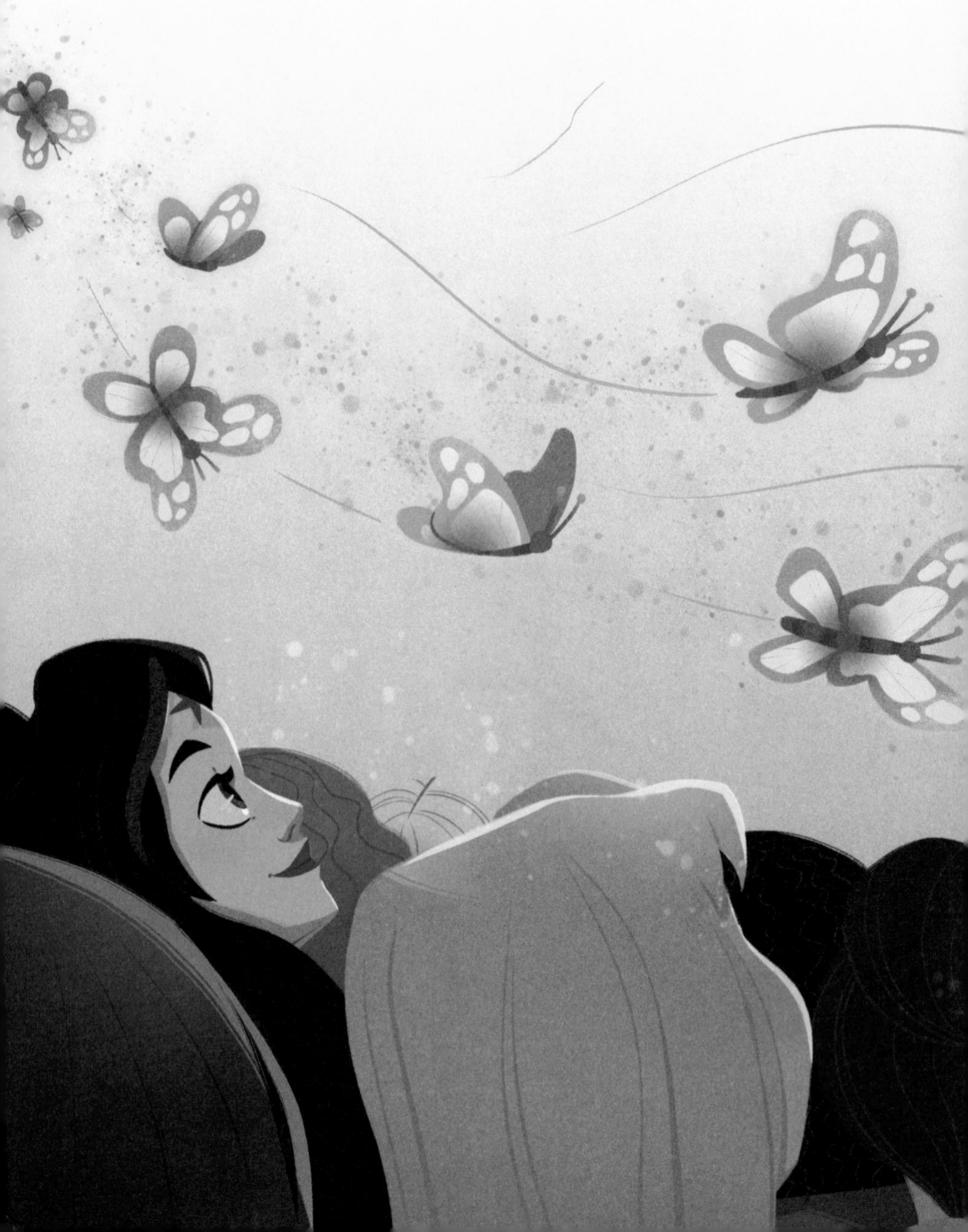

They were more incredible than
the heroes had imagined!
They sparkled in the sun
like jewels.

Suddenly, the Save the Day Alarm rang!
Bumblebee pointed to a giant bug
in the sky.

"That's the *Mothwing*!"

Batgirl said.

"And that means Killer Moth!

Get ready for trouble."

Killer Moth's ship sprayed thin white strands over the crowd. The stuff was sticky!

"Help!" people cried.

The more they struggled,

the more tangled they became.

The *Mothwing* landed.
Killer Moth stepped out
with a large net.
He began scooping up
the butterflies!

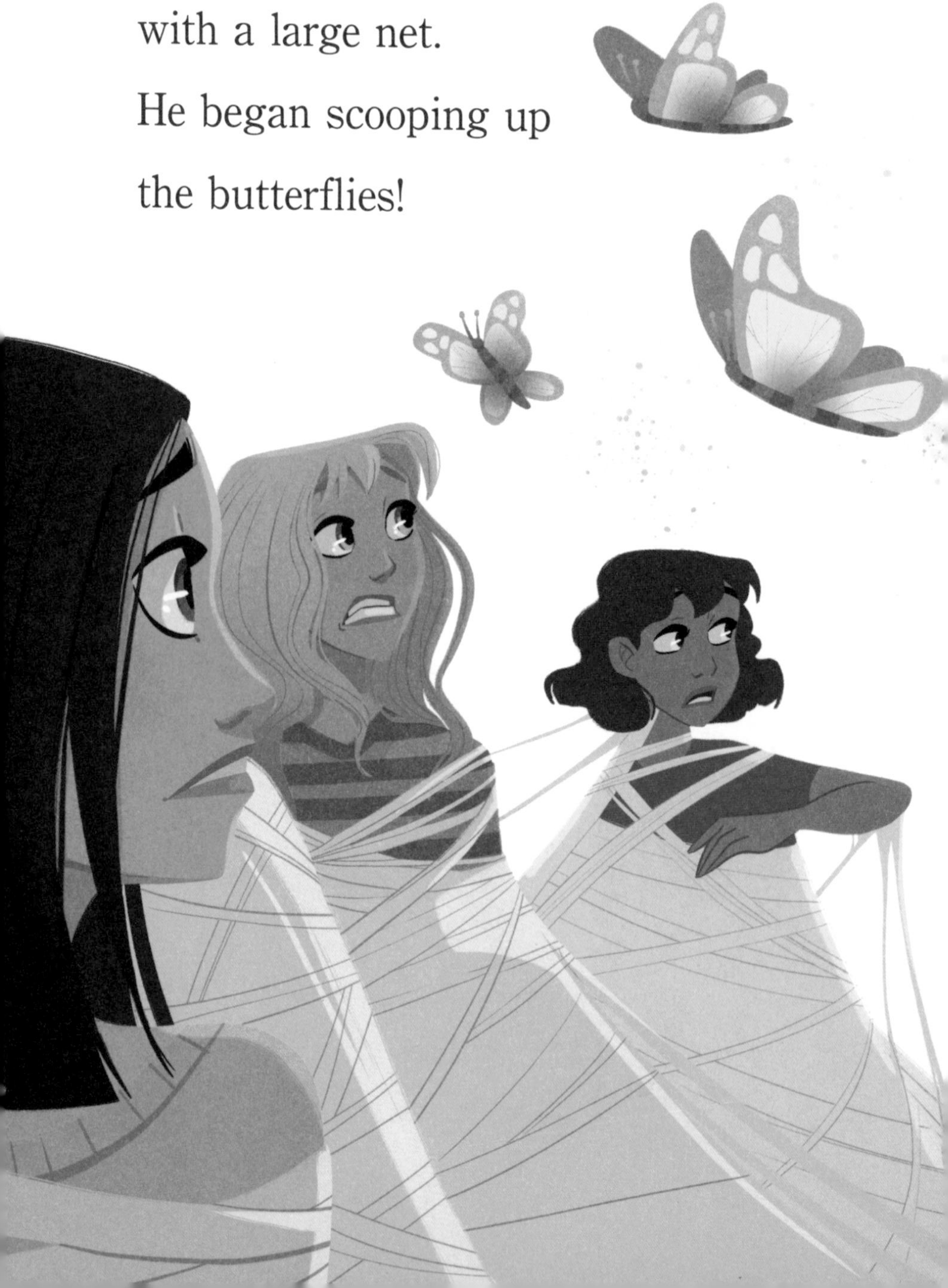

"The secrets of the
space monarchs
will be mine!"
the villain cheered.

Batgirl quietly reached
into her Utility Belt.
She cut the heroes loose.

"Help free the others,"
Bumblebee whispered
to her friends.
"I have a plan."

Bumblebee shrank to bee size
and hid among the butterflies.

Killer Moth didn't see her.

He scooped her right up

into his net!

"Oh, my little friends," Killer Moth whispered when his net was full. "I need to know how you survive in outer space.

"Then I can make a super suit
one thousand times more powerful
than any of those heroes!"

"Not so fast!" Bumblebee yelled.
Growing back to her normal size,
she ripped through the net.
Then she used her blasters
to blow the plane door open.

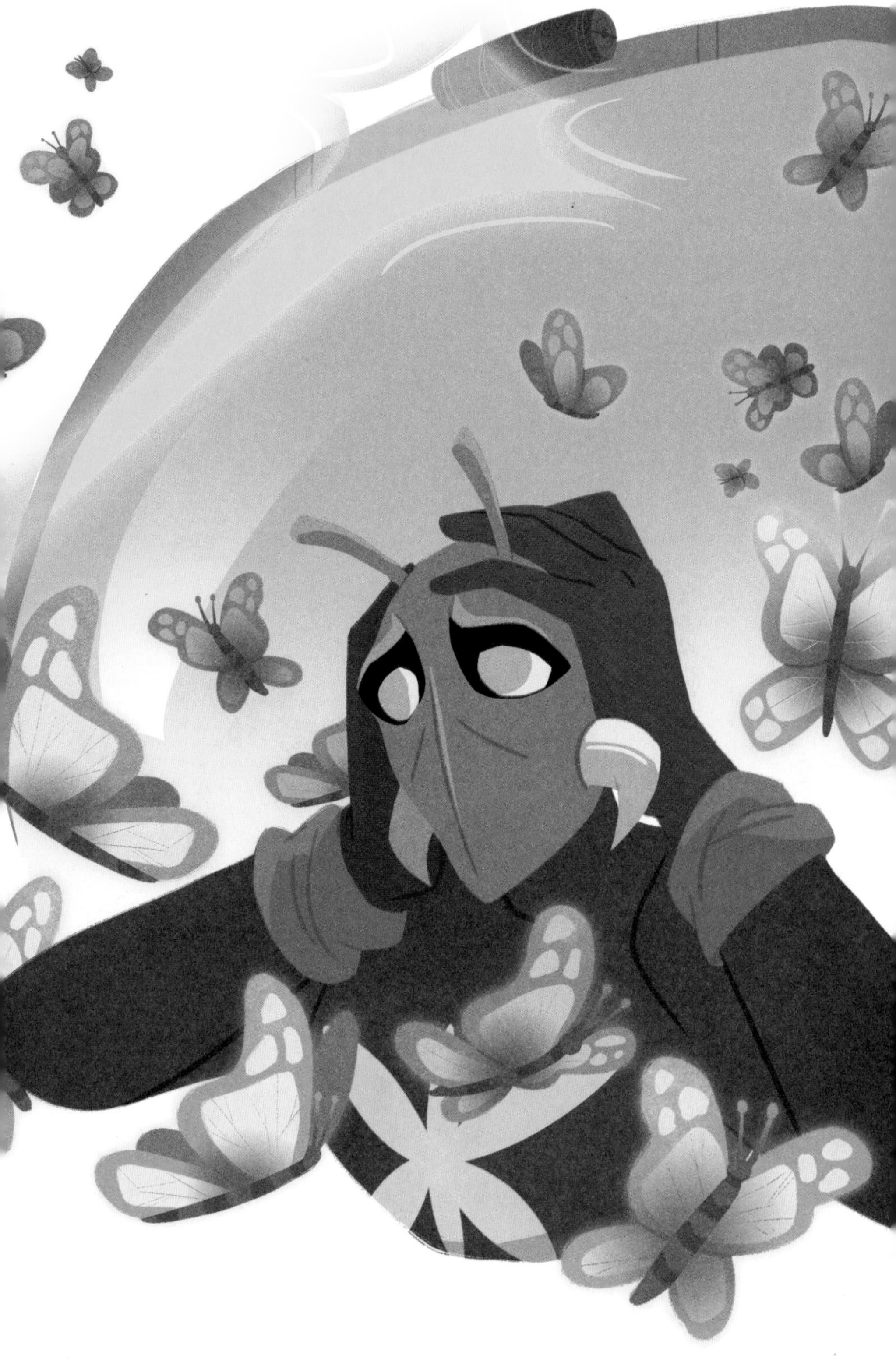

Wonder Woman pulled out
her Lasso of Truth.
Batgirl prepared a net.
They were ready for action!

The butterflies flew free
from the ship.

Bumblebee and Killer Moth
came crashing out
of the *Mothwing*.

Batgirl did a backflip

and swung her net.

Wonder Woman tied
the villain tight
with her lasso!

"Excellent save, team,"

Principal Waller said.

"I'm nominating you all for . . .

"Hero of the *Moth*!"
Everyone laughed
as the monarchs
returned to the stars.